Ronaldio Donaldio

Ever since the World Cup started, everyone in school has been comperleeterly into football.

— FWOOSH! —

Like the other Saturday when my best friend Bunky was playing keepy uppy in Mogden Park.

totes showing off

'A hundred and seventy seven, a hundred and seventy eight, a hundred and seventy nine . . .' he counted, showing off how many times he could do it.

Barry Loser is the best at football

NOT!

Half-time oranges chopped by

Jim Smith

'Pull the other one, Bunkoid,' burped Darren Darrenofski, slurping on a can of World Cup flavour Fronkle. 'Even Ronaldio Donaldio can't do it that many times!'

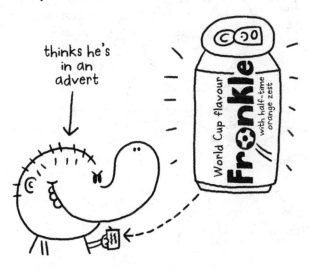

thinks he's in an advert

World Cup flavour **Fronkle** with half-time orange zest

Ronaldio Donaldio is the keelest footballer in the whole wide world amen. He plays for the Smeldovian football team, who everyone reckons are going to win the World Cup easily.

'Ronaldio Donaldio?' sniggled Nancy, looking up from the book she was reading. 'That's the stupidest name I've ever heard!'

Sharonella leaned her head on Nancy's shoulder like she was a parrot. 'Oh my days Nance,' she squawked. 'You trying to tell me you've never heard of Ronaldio Donaldio?'

isn't parrot in real life

Nancy shrugged. 'I'm just not that into football,' she said.

'You don't know what you're missing, babes!' said Sharonella, whipping a football card out of her pocket.

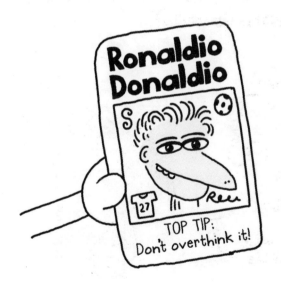

Ronaldio Donaldio

27

TOP TIP: Don't overthink it!

Gordon Smugly sidled up with his sort-of-servant, Stuart Shmendrix. 'Ronaldio Donaldio?' he said. 'Yeah, he's alright I spose.'

Gordon

Stuart

'Think you're pretty good then, do you?' said a voice from behind us, and I turned round.

Standing in front of me were
five really tall, smug-looking kids
wearing shiny green football kits.
On the front of their T-shirts were
the words 'Green Giants'.

like this

Darren crumpled an empty Fronkle
can in one hand and kicked it
towards a bin. It flew straight over
and donked a squirrel off a branch.

'Who are you lot when you're at home?' barked Darren as the squirrel limped off.

already planning revenge

'We're the Green Giants,' said the kid at the front whose blonde hair was combed so neatly it looked like Nancy's open book. He pointed at his T-shirt. 'Can't you Mogden losers read?'

Stuart Shmendrix pointed at Nancy. 'We can read,' he said. 'Look, she's reading right now.'

'Whatever,' said the kid next to the blonde one. 'Come on Tarquin, let's get out of here - it stinks!'

Tarquin

'That's cos of Mogden Sewage Works?' said Sharonella, as if that was a good thing. 'The smell blows over this way when the wind's going in the right direction?'

the right direction →

'Delightful,' chuckled Tarquin. 'Of course, we don't have that problem up in Avocado Hill.'

What is Avocado Hill?

Avocado Hill is the posh little village that sits on top of a slope overlooking Mogden Town.

You are now entering **Avocado Hill**
Look down on Mogden Town!

Tarquin dropped the ball he was holding and kicked it back up with his foot, ducking to catch it on the back of his neck, then flicking his head to make it bounce into his hands again.

'Pretty impressive,' said Nancy. 'And I don't even like football.'

Tarquin turned to Bunky. 'I was watching you keepy uppying,' he said. 'Not bad for a Mogdener.'

'Fanks!' grinned Bunky, who thinks he's the best at football out of all of us, probably cos he is.

didn't actukeely get this

BEST PLAYER EVER

'Tell you what,' said Tarquin. 'We've got a little stadium up in Avo Hill - nothing fancy, just a few hundred seats. You lot fancy a game next Saturday, after the World Cup final?'

Bunky looked at the ball in Tarquin's hands and gulped. 'Oh, er . . . I'm busy then,' he said.

'Me too,' squawked Sharonella. 'I'm going to the, um . . . toilet.'

'With me!' burped Darren, putting his hand up in the air.

Gordon pulled his phone out of his pocket. 'Do you know what,' he said, tapping the screen. 'I'm fully booked for the next three weeks.'

just looking at selfies

'He's my boss,' said Stuart, pointing at Smugly. 'So looks like I'll be tied up as well.'

I looked round at my friends.
'How come I didn't know about
all these plans?' I said.

Tarquin peered down at me. 'You're
a funny little specimen, aren't you?'
he chuckled.

Tarquin's
shnozzle

'What's that sposed to mean?'
I asked.

The kid next to Tarquin rolled his
eyes. 'Your pals are making excuses,'
he explained. 'They're just afraid to
play the Green Giants.'

You know when you're the last person to work something out and it makes you feel all stupid, so you say something cocky to make yourself look keel?

'We'll see you on Saturday,' I said, twizzling round to face the Green Giants. 'And we're gonna smash you avocados into a paste!'

available at Feeko's

Picking the team

The Green Giants wandered off and Bunky glared at me. 'What in the name of unkeelness was that all about?' he cried.

'What are you afraid of, Bunky?' I said, pretending it was no big deal. 'I thought you were the best footballer in Mogden School!'

'I spose that IS true,' said Bunky.

'But we don't even have a team,' warbled Stuart.

'Well then,' I said, still trying to make up for looking like a loser three minutes earlier. 'We'd better make one!'

Bunky stroked the bit of his face where his beard'll be when he's older. 'Hmm, let me see,' he said. 'I'd be up front, of keelse. Darren, you can go in midfield. Shazza and Stuart in defence and Gordon in goal.'

'Wait a millisecond,' I said. 'What about me and Nancy?'

'Leave me out of this,' said Nancy, not even looking up from her book.

this is not Tarquin's hair

'You don't want to play do you, Barry?' asked Bunky.

Darren cracked open another Fronkle. 'Yeah Loser,' he said. 'You're rubbish at football!'

'No I'm not!' I said, even though it was true. I scratched my head, and my brain wriggled inside its skull, immedikeely coming up with one of its amazekeel ideas.

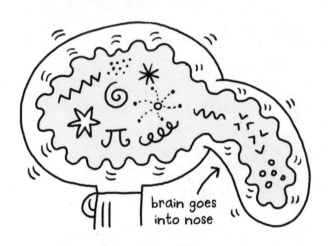

brain goes into nose

'I've got it!' I cried. 'I can be your **football coach!**'

Coach Loser

'You have got to be kidding,' laughed Gordon.

Darren took a slurp of Fronkle. 'Forgeddaboudit, Loser,' he belched.

'Oh **PLEEEASE**,' I said, immedikeely losing my keelness and dropping to my knees. 'Don't leave me on the sidelines with nobody to talk to!'

too much?

Nancy looked up from her book. 'Ahem?' she ahemed.

'No offence, Nance,' I said, peering up at Bunky. 'What d'you reckon, Captain?' I smiled, calling him that so he'd go along with my plan.

Bunky ruffled my hair like I was his son. 'It's a nice idea, Baz, but you don't actukeely know anything about football, do you?'

'That fact might be ever-so-slighterly true,' I said, getting up off my knees. 'But I'm pretty good at bossing people about!'

me off my knees

'And you think that's all it takes to be a coach?' said Gordon.

'Oui,' I said, showing off I could say 'yes' in French, because I've been learning it in school.

Sharonella's nose crinkled up. 'Urgh, we don't need to hear about your toilet habits, Barry!' she said.

wee ✗
oui ✓

'Yeah, Losoid,' said Darren. 'Nice idea about the team, but I don't think we'll be needing your services, okay?'

'Right that's it,' I said, stomping my foot and preparing to activate **Operation Pain au Chocolat**. 'I didn't want to do this, but it looks like I'm gonna have to.'

Operation Pain au Chocolat

I rotated myself on the spot like a tray of pain au chocolats in a bakery shop window and walked away from my ex-friends.

like this

I was putting on a fake limp to make them feel extra sorry for me.

'Oh don't be like that, Barry!' called Bunky.

'No you're right,' I mumbled over my shoulder. 'What do you lot need a useless old Loser like me for?'

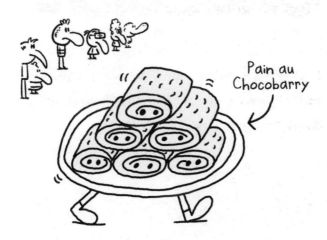

Pain au Chocobarry

'Just let him go, Bunky,' said Gordon Smugly, who's always trying to steal my best friend off me and probably thought this was the perfect time to put his evil plan into action.

I spotted a piece of gravel lying on the floor and wondered if I should fake a trip over it to really get them feeling bad.

'I'll be alright,' I mumbled. 'Don't you worry about Barry Loser, he'll get over it in a couple of weeks or so.'

I carried limping off for a couple of milliseconds until I heard Sharonella's mouth opening.

impressed with my hearing?

'"Coach Loser",' she said, trying the name out for size. 'I suppose it has got a tiny bit of a ring to it . . .'

I chuckled to myself. 'The old Pain-au-Choc trick never fails,' I muttered, widening my earholes by 0.3 millimetres each, trying to hear if anyone was nodding their head to what Shaz just said.

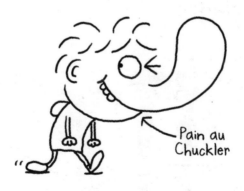

Pain au Chuckler

But heads nodding aren't as easy to hear as mouths opening.

I carried on facing away from my friends. 'What do you reckon, Bunk?' I croaked, shortening Bunky's name to show Gordon Smugly how much of his best friend I was. 'How about doing an old pal a favour?'

Everything went quiet for a billisecond.

'Oh alright,' sighed Bunky, as his bum started to cry.

waaah!

Crying Freakoids

'Hey, you alright, little fella?' said Bunky, pulling a Crying Freakoid out of his pocket.

Crying Freakoids are the latest craze at school - apart from football, of keelse. They're these tiny football-shaped toys which sort of act like pets you have to look after.

They're the size of a gobstopper with batteries inside and a mini speaker on the back. On the front are little screens with faces on them that show what mood the ball's in.

Crying
Freakoid

Whenever one starts to cry or act unhappy at all, the owner has to work out if it's hungry or needs the toilet or wants a little cuddle to make it feel better.

'Hey that's a point, better check in with Barry Junior,' I said, pulling my Crying Freakoid out of my pocket.

I held Barry Junior up and looked at his face. His eyes were scrunched shut and his mouth was grimacing.

waaaah!

'Argh, I think that means he needs a poo!' I cried.

'You'd better wipe his bum then, Baz,' said Shaz, pulling her Crying Freakoid out of her pocket.

I scraped my finger along the bottom of my Crying Freakoid, which is what you're supposed to do when they need the toilet. Barry Junior did a happy beep and his grimace turned into a smile.

'I don't know what you lot see in those things,' said Nancy. 'Looks like a lot of hard work to me.'

'Oh it is,' said Stuart, all seriously.

Stuart's Crying Freakoid is called Stuey No Legs. It was sitting in the palm of his hand doing a sad face, which meant he'd have to sing to it to make it happy.

'It's really rewarding once you get used to it though,' he sang, and Stuey No Legs did a grin.

'Stuart's right, I can't imagine not having my Mini Shaz,' said Sharonella, giving hers a peck. 'And they grow up so fast, don't they!'

SMACK!

Bunky, whose Crying Freakoid is called Bunky Two, nodded. 'Life's never the same once you've had one of these little critters,' he sniggled. He patted Bunky Two on the head and it immedikeely stopped crying.

'Uh-oh, looks like somebody's hungry,' said Gordon, pointing at his Freakoid. Its mouth was wide open, digital drool dripping out of it.

He poked his finger at the mouth bit, which is what you do when one of them needs feeding. 'There, that's better isn't it, Lil Gordy?' he cooed.

'Ugh, I can't take any more of this,' said Nancy, slamming her book shut. 'I think I'll go and find something more interesting to do.'

SLAM!

'It's your life, Verkenwerken!' shouted Darren as she wandered off, and he whipped Dazzy Rascal out of his pocket. Its eyes were closed and it purred quietly.

'Ooh you are lucky Daz,' whispered Shazza. 'Wish my one'd sleep through like that.'

'It was a different story last night Shaz,' yawned Darren. 'I was up with him every two hours.'

bags under his eyes

'Worth it though, innit,' I said, sounding like my mum when she talks to her mum-friends about my baby brother Desmond.

The sun was going down and my nose twitched, sniffing the smell of my dinner wafting over from my house, mixed in with the stench of Mogden Sewers.

mini Baz inside shnoz

'I'll see you lot bright and early Monday morning,' I said, plopping Barry Junior in my pocket. 'If we're gonna beat those Green Giants we've got a lot of work to do!'

No banana

Suddenkeely it was Monday morning and we were all standing in the playground at school.

'First things first,' I said, clapping my hands together. 'We need a team name.'

'Ooh you should be good at this Bazzy,' said Shaz. 'You're always coming up with stupid names for stuff!'

'Thank you Sharonella,' I said, thinking back on all the amazekeel names I've come up with since I've been alive, including for my nine hamsters, all of which are now comperleeterly dead.

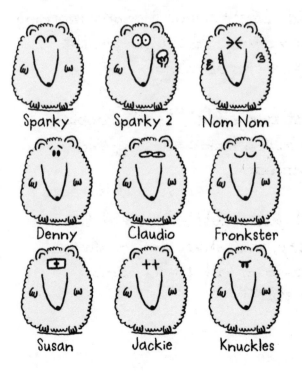

Sparky

Sparky 2

Nom Nom

Denny

Claudio

Fronkster

Susan

Jackie

Knuckles

'How about The Darrens?'
said Darren, and I scoffed.

'Nice try, Darrenofski,' I said.
'But no banana.'

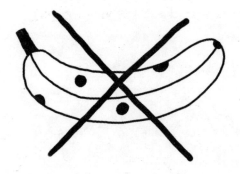

'Gordon's Giants?' said Gordon,
and Shazza shook her head.

'That sounds exackerly like
Green Giants,' she said.

'Yeah, expect it's Gordon's
instead of Green,' snapped Gordon.

'Guys, guys, guys,' I said in my Coach Loser voice, which is just my normal, regular voice. 'Let's try and support each other's ideas, shall we?'

Bunky scratched his no-beard.

SCRITCH

SCRATCH

'The Mogden Maniacs?' he said, and I clicked my fingers.

Mogden Maniacs

'I've got it!' I cried. 'The Mogden Maniacs.'

'That's what I said,' muttered Bunky.

'Is it?' I said. 'Well shall we just go with my idea instead?'

Bunky squinted, his tiny little brain
getting all confused. 'Erm, o-kay . . .'
he said. 'We should probably get on
with some practice anyway.'

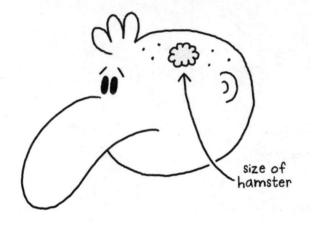

size of
hamster

'Good point, Captain,' I said.
'Everybody drop and give me
a hundred.'

'A hundred what?' asked Stuart.

'Press-ups, of keelse,' I grinned.

'Why don't you give **ME** a hundred press-ups?' said Darren, as Bunky got on the ground and started pumping his arms up and down.

'Good boy, Captain!' I smiled, wondering if I was overdoing the whole Captain thing a bit.

'One, two, three . . .' he panted, his face going red.

Sharonella joined in. 'That's the spirit, Shaz!' I boomed. 'Shmendrix, Smugly - don't hold back. You too, Darrenofski!'

Stuart and his sort-of boss dropped to their knees next to Shazza. 'One, two ...' gasped Gordon. 'I'm doing this for the TEAM ... three, four ... not for YOU, Loser!'

'That's COACH Loser to you,' I said.

'If you say that one more time...'
said Darren, not finishing his
sentence.

'Right, that's a hundred more
press-ups for you, Darrenofski,'
I shouted. 'What are you, a
Maniac or a mouse?'

I was really beginning to get into
this being a coach thing.

Darren looked down at the b
his hands. 'You want me to act like
a maniac?' he asked.

'Yes please,' I smiled.

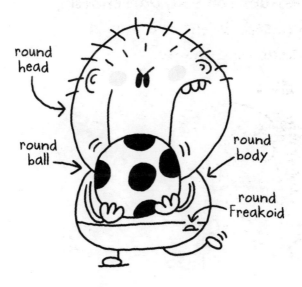

And he booted the ball right at
my shnozzle.

Queenie down

'Argh, my prize-winning hooter!'
I screamed, as the football boinked
off my nose and into the air.

The ball arched across the sky like
a sped-up mini-moon.

'Heads up, Queenie!' cried a freckly little kiddywinkle, and I Pain-au-Choc'ed round to see Queenie, Mogden School's head dinner lady.

Not that me and my friends call our dinner ladies 'dinner ladies', we call them 'dinner dames' because it's keeler.

Queenie

Queenie is three hundred years old,
the height of a bollard and needs
a walking stick to get around.
But that doesn't stop everyone
being comperleeterly afraid of her.

She's married to Mr Walbyoff, the
school caretaker who's been working
on a doll's-house-sized model of Mogden
for the last eight trillion years that
he keeps on display in the school foyer.

Mr Walbyoff

I think he only does it to get away
from Queenie.

The ball was still speeding through the air, by the way.

'What's that?' growled Queenie, turning her head round as a ball-shaped shadow crept across her face.

I scrunched my eyes shut for a
billisecond, opening them to see
a circle of kiddywinkles standing
round a knocked-over bollard
wearing a grey wig. Then I realised
it was Queenie.

Queenie's wrinkly eyelids fluttered
open like a million-year-old butterfly
stretching its wings after a
particukeely long snooze, and the
kiddywinkles screamed.

Queenie grabbed her stick and pulled herself back up to bollard-height. 'Which one of you little brats bonked Queenie on the bonce?' she squawked.

I rotated myself on the spot like an out-of-date tray of pain au chocs. 'Psst, Bunky!' I whispered, my back to Queenie now. 'Is she looking at me?'

'One hundred!' gasped Bunky, as I felt a walking stick tap me on the shoulder.

Queenie's drawer

I twizzled myself round at 0.2 millimetres per hour until I was face to face with Queenie's face.

'That little lassie tells me it was this little Loser what knocked old Queenie down,' she said, pointing over her shoulder at the freckly kiddywinkle from earlier.

what's this kiddywinkle's problemo?

'I-it was a mistake Queenie,' I stuttered, as my pocket started to cry.

'What's that noise?' asked Queenie, turning the dials up on her hearing aids.

My body turned to stone and a zig-zag of fear crackled through it, breaking me into a billion bits of glued-together gravel.

'N-nothing,' I said, trying to suck my pocket in so she wouldn't spot the Crying Freakoid.

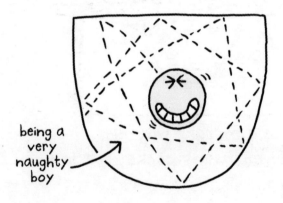

being a very naughty boy

I'd seen Queenie confiscate people's prized possessions before, and I didn't want it happening to me.

Rumour had it she locked them inside
a ginormous drawer hidden away
somewhere in a cold, dark corner of
the staff room. And once something
went inside that drawer, it never
came out again.

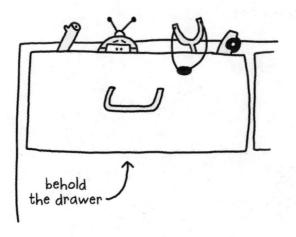

behold
the drawer

'Nothing eh?' said Queenie, waggling
her nostrils. 'Doesn't sound like
nothing to me.'

I looked at Queenie's hearing aids and thought how lucky she was her nostrils didn't have smelling aids in them too, because I'd just blown off.

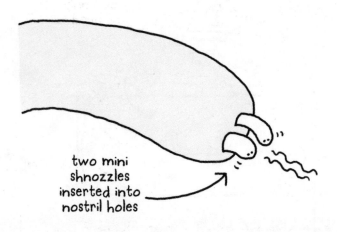

two mini
shnozzles
inserted into
nostril holes

'I hope for your sake it isn't one of those Cry-y Freaky thingys,' she warbled. 'You know they've been banned in school, don't you, laddie?'

A clip-clopping noise got louder
and louder then stopped. Dolly,
the nicest, fattest dinner dame
in Mogden School, had appeared
behind Queenie.

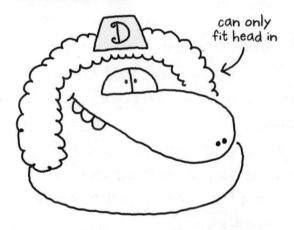

can only
fit head in

'Everything alright over here?'
she smiled, and Queenie blinked.

'Yep,' she snapped, not even looking
at Dolly. I peered at the two dinner
dames, standing there like a couple of
bollards that'd been concreted into
the pavement too close together.

65

'I was just having a little word with Loser here about the importance of not bonking head dinner ladies on the, er . . . head,' said Queenie.

Dolly winked at me. 'I'm sure Barry's got the message,' she said. 'Barry, have you got the message?'

'Ping!' I said, doing the noise of a phone getting a message, and Queenie scrunched up her already scrunched-up face.

'I'm watching you, Loser!' she shouted, hobbling off in the direction of a kiddywinkle picking daisies. 'And don't you forget it!'

Home time

The bell clanged and we all headed back into school. I watched the clock tick its way to half past three, patting my pocket every few minutes to keep Barry Junior quiet.

And then it was home time.

'Off you go, you blooming Maniacs!'
I said at the top of my road. 'And
remember to get a good night's
sleep - we've got a lot of work to
do tomorrow.'

'Whatevoids, Loser,' burped Darren.

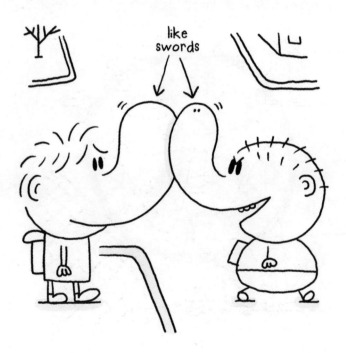

like
swords

'That's another ten press-ups for you, Darrenofski!' I shouted in my jokey voice.

It's important as a football coach to have a bit of fun with your team at the end of a hard day.

that squirrel

'See ya later Daddio,' said Bunky,
strolling off without giving me a
triple-reverse-upside-down-salute,
which is what he usually does.

'Not if I see you first, Captain!'
I called back, hoping all this Captain
business wasn't going to his head.

I walked up to my house, put the
key in the door, turned it, pushed
the door open and stepped into
the hallway.

Sozzles about how boring that last
sentence was, by the way.

'Oo-ooh love!' cooed my mum as I forward-rolled into the living room, the way my favourite TV star, Future Ratboy, would.

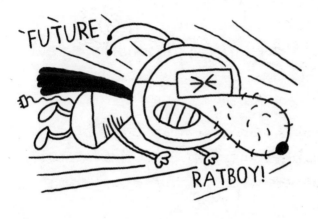

FUTURE

RATBOY!

'Afternoon Mumsicles,' I called back, jumping onto the sofa and clicking the telly on.

'Bawwy!' gurgled my baby brother Desmond, stumbling into the room. 'You wanna pway wiv me?'

I ruffled Des's hair like he was my kid brother, which he is. 'Not now, Dezzy,' I smiled. 'Your big bruv's had a busy day. He's a football coach now, did you know that?'

Des stared at me, drool dripping out of his mouth like a Crying Freakoid at feeding time.

Just then the front door opened. 'Oo-ooh!' called my dad and I looked at Des, doing my 'What's Dad doing home this early?' face.

Loser family laptop

'What are you doing home this early, Dad?' I said, turning my face into a sentence, and he slumped into the chair next to me.

'Ugh, I've been on one of these blooming team-building courses with work,' he groaned. 'Only good thing about 'em is they finish early.'

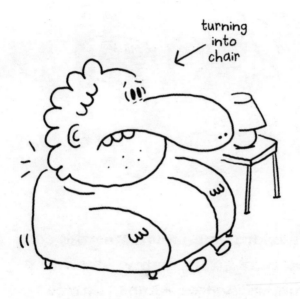

turning into chair

'Mm,' I said, comperleeterly bored with what he was talking about already.

My mum walked into the room
with a tray of Feeko's chocolate
digestives. 'Ooh how was it, Kenneth?'
she asked.

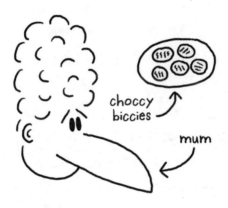

choccy
biccies

mum

I closed my eyes, wondering why
they were still nattering about
something so yawnsome. 'Do you
mind?' I said. 'I'm trying to
concentrate - we've got a big
game coming up on Saturday.'

'A big game?' said my dad. 'What's all this about, Barry?'

'Well,' I said. 'Tarquin from the Green Giants challenged us to a showdown in Avocado Hill. Only problem was, Bunky and the team didn't think I was up to it. Then I activated Operation Pain au Chocolat and – hey presto – looks like I'm the Mogden Maniacs' coach!'

all proud

'O-kaay,' said my dad, looking like he didn't know what in the keelness I was talking about.

He grabbed the remote control out of my lap and flicked the telly onto the football channel.

ROAR!

'Yeah, I've signed us up against the Green Giants this Saturday,' I carried on. 'So I've really got my work cut out!'

'Uh-huh,' mumbled my dad, staring at the screen.

Smeldovia, who wear yellow outfits, were playing a team in blue. 'And here comes Donaldio!' boomed the commentator through the television's speakers.

Ronaldio Donaldio!

I zoomed my eyes in, spotting Ronaldio Donaldio kicking a ball towards the goal. 'He nutmegs Guacamole, takes it past the defenders,' roared the commentator. 'Stops . . . shoots . . .'

'GOAL!'

cried my dad, and the TV cut to a shot of the Smeldovian team's coach jumping up and down on the sidelines, cheering and shouting at his players.

'Hmm, that gives me an idea,' I muttered to myself, reaching across to the coffee table and grabbing the Loser family laptop.

Smoogle

I opened the lid of the laptop,
clicked on the internet and typed
'www.smoogle.com' into the bar
at the top.

Smoogle, in case you didn't know, is the keelest search engine in the whole wide world wide web amen. It was invented by Wolf Tizzler, who's this child genius that's sort of like me but with frizzier hair and glasses.

Wolf Tizzler

Once I was on the Smoogle page I tapped the words 'Smeldovian coach' into its search bar, pressed enter, and a whole page of photos flashed up on the screen.

'Smeldovian coaches are amongst the most dangerous and dilapidated in the world,' read a caption underneath a picture of a scuffed-up brown and orange one.

clicker
arrow

I ignored that photo and clicked on one of a man who looked pretty much exackerly like the person I'd just seen on the telly.

The laptop screen went blank for a billisecond, then a bright yellow page popped up:

Welcome to the official website of the Smeldovian football team's world famous coach, Chip Snyder!

TOP TIPS:
1. No distractions
2. Keep fit

'Now we're talking!' I said, immedi-clicking on Chip Snyder's Top Tips.

Coach Loser's nursery for Crying Freakoids

'Mornkeels, team!' I yawned in the playground the next morning.

Barry Junior had kept me up half the night crying his head off, but I was still looking forward to putting some of Chip Snyder's Top Tips into action.

I held up an empty shoebox I'd brought from home and gave it a waggle, waiting for someone to ask me what it was for.

'Yo, yo, yo, Coach Loser in da house!' grinned Bunky, bouncing the official Mogden Maniacs football off his knee and booting it to Darren.

looks like two Ws when upside down

'Good to see you, Captain,' I said, wondering when we'd be getting back to calling each other by our normal, everyday names.

Jocelyn Twiggs from my class tapped me on the shoulder. 'Hey Bazza, are you the lot who's playing the Green Giants in Avocado Hill this Saturday?' he asked.

Jocelyn
Twiggs

'Yeah, what's it got to do with you, Twiggs?' burped Darren.

I put my hand up to calm Darren down. 'That's right, Jossy,' I said. 'How'd you know about that?'

'They've put posters up all round town,' said Jocelyn. 'Big, shiny, colourful ones too. Must've cost a fortune.'

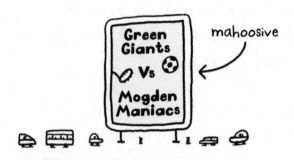

'Gulp,' said Sharonella.

Nancy strolled over with a tape measure in her hand. 'How's it going, Coach?' she chuckled.

'Nothing a bit of hard work can't sort out,' I said, as she wrapped her tape measure round the trunk of a nearby tree.

'Erm, what in the name of playing it unkeel are you doing?' I said, waggling my shoe box in the air.

I was beginning to get ever so slighterly annoyed that nobody had noticed it yet.

'Oh this?' said Nancy, jotting something down in a notebook. 'I've joined the Miniature Mogden Voluntary Measurement Committee.'

what's she talking about?

I stared at Nancy like she was speaking in Smeldovian. 'Exkizzy mizzy?' I said, showing off I could say 'excuse me' in Smeldovian.

'I'm measuring stuff for Mr Walbyoff's doll's house project,' explained Nancy. 'I write down the size in this book then divide it by a hundred. That way Mr Walbyoff knows how small to make the models.'

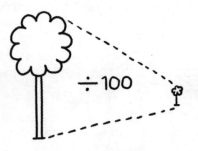

$\div 100$

'It's your life,' I said, as Gordon Smugly and his sort-of-servant ambled up.

'What's that shoe box for, Coach Loser?' asked Stuart.

'Thank you Stuart,' I said, relieved somebody had FINALLY noticed it. 'Okay team, gather round - I've got something to say.'

The Maniacs all gathered round and I looked each one of them in the eye, the way Chip Snyder tells you to in his Top Tip number twelve.

'Here's the deal, people,' I said, snatching Mini Shaz out of Sharonella's hand. 'From now on I'll be looking after your Crying Freakoids.'

'Wha?!' cried Shazza, not finishing her 'what'. 'B-but you can't take my Mini Shaz away from me like that!'

I plopped Mini Shaz into the shoe box and held my hand out for everyone else's. 'Come on, Captain,' I said, clicking my fingers, and Bunky slow-motion-handed me Bunky Two.

'What's this all about, Bus?' he asked.

'"Bus"?' I said. 'Why in the unkeeness are you calling me "Bus"?'

Bunky chuckled. 'I thought it up last night,' he said, giving himself a mini-reverse-salute. 'What's like a "Coach" but not as good? A **BUS** - get it!'

last night, chuckling to self

'I like it, Bunk!' sniggled Gordon, and I bit my lip, trying to remember Chip Snyder's Top Tip number seventy-nine, which is this: 'Don't get all jealous when Gordon's trying to steal your best friend'.

Or maybe that's just one of mine.

'Two words,' I said, pincering Dazzy Rascal out of Darren's pocket and placing it next to the other Crying Freakoids. 'Chip Snyder.'

PLOP AGAIN!

'Chip Snyder?' said Gordon. 'Isn't that the Smeldovian football coach?'

I nodded. 'Yep, turns out he's got a list of Top Tips on his website,' I smiled, as Stuart handed me Stuey No Legs. 'And number one is "No distractions" - which is why I'm confiscating your Crying Freakoids.'

The bell for lessons started clanging and Gordon's mouth opened, getting ready to say something annoying.

'Save it for later, Smugly,' I snapped, grabbing Lil Gordy and plonking him in the official Mogden Maniacs shoe box.

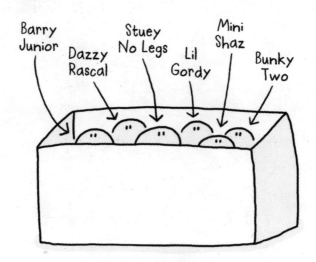

Barry Junior

Dazzy Rascal

Stuey No Legs

Lil Gordy

Mini Shaz

Bunky Two

Plurgle Flurgle

I don't know if you've ever tried keeping a shoe box-full of Crying Freakoids quiet for a whole morning's lessons, but it's not as easy as it sounds.

'Psst, Bazzy!' whispered Sharonella, leaning over from her desk.

Miss Spivak was at the front of the class, warbling on about the history of Mogden Sewage Works.

Miss Spivak

'How's Mini Shaz doing?' hissed Maxi Shaz.

'FINE,' I whispered, peeping between my feet where the shoe box was sitting inside my half-unzipped rucksack. 'Just keep it shtum, would you Shazza? The last thing we need is Miss Spivak confiscating this lot.'

'Enjoying fatherhood, Barry?' giggled Nancy, who was sitting on the other side of me.

'Shouldn't you be measuring something?' I yawned. I was really beginning to feel sleepy now.

like two Freakoids smooching in a swimming pool

Nancy whipped her measuring tape out. 'Would it actually be that bad, getting your Crying Freakoid confiscated?' she whisper-asked, jotting down the width of her desk. 'Surely it'd be a break from all that whining?'

Lil Gordy started whimpering and I lifted him out of my bag. 'Don't you know anything?' I whispered. 'If you leave one of these little fellas alone for too long they'll DIE!'

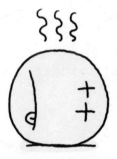

Nancy shrugged. 'I can think of worse things that could happen,' she muttered.

'You're a monster, Verkenwerken,' mumbled Darren, who was slumped over his desk, half asleep.

I held Lil Gordy up to my face and gave him a kiss to keep him quiet.

'Bleurgh, he tastes of Smugly's pocket!' I spluttered, a teeny-weeny bit too loudly.

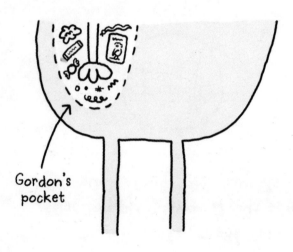

Gordon's pocket

Miss Spivak squinted her eyes, peering across the room at me. 'Everything alright, Loser?' she asked.

'Yes Miss Spivak,' I said, faking a few more splutters. 'M-must be how well you're teaching us about sewers - it's, erm, almost like I can smell the actual real-life poos and wees!'

virtual reality style

'Oh,' said Miss Spivak. 'Yes, well I'm glad I'm getting it across so . . . vividly.'

'Oi, what're you trying to say about my pockets, Barold?' whispered Gordon from behind me.

'I think he's saying they smell like sewers,' said Stuart, but not in a horrible way, just like it was a fact.

pongkets

'Hey, Barry?' he carried on.

'What is it, Shmendrix?' I said, as quietly as possible.

'It's the football game,' whispered Stuart, doing a blow off against his plastic seat. It echoed round the classroom and everybody apart from Miss Spivak sniggled. 'It's playing havoc with my nerves.'

PARP!

I rolled my eyes. 'Can we PERLEASE talk about this at break?' I said, looking up at the clock on the wall – it was almost eleven.

Bunky tapped me on the shoulder.
'How's Bunky Two doing, Bus?'
he said.

'Stop calling me that!'

I hissed.

'Loser!' shouted Miss Spivak. 'What are you jabbering on about now?'

I plunked Lil Gordy back into my bag. 'Oh I was just saying to Nigel here how interesting this lesson was. Isn't that right, Zuckerberg?'

Nigel Zuckerberg is Bunky's real-life name, by the way. And he **HATES** being called it.

Bunky squinted at me. 'That's right, **BUS**,' he said through his clenched-together teeth.

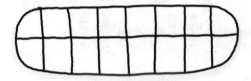

'Something's going on here,' muttered Miss Spivak to herself, putting her pen down and scraping out of her chair. She clip-clopped down the aisle towards me. 'What's that wailing noise, Loser?' she said, getting closer.

I closed my knees together, trying to muffle the crying sound wafting out of my rucksack.

'Waaah, waaah,' I cried, not exackerly sure what my plan was, but hoping one would pop into my head soon.

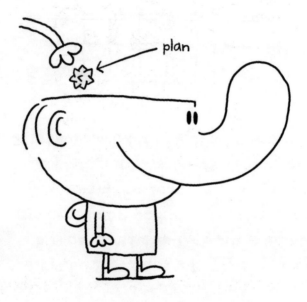

plan

Miss Spivak stopped clip-clopping. 'Are you crying, Barry?' she asked.

Sharonella gave me a sneaky wink, like she was coming up with one of her use-er-less ideas.

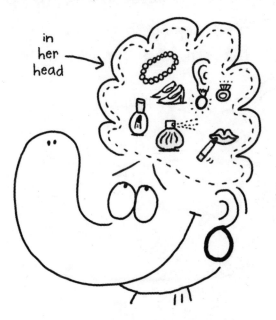

in her head

'There there, Bazzy,' she cooed, sliding her arm round my shoulders. 'Don't tell me you haven't heard, Miss?'

Miss Spivak blinked. 'Heard what?' she asked, looking suspicious.

'Poor old Barry's had some terrible news this morning,' said Sharonella. 'Yeah, his . . .' she stopped talking for a millisecond, trying to think of what to say. 'His erm, hamster died again?'

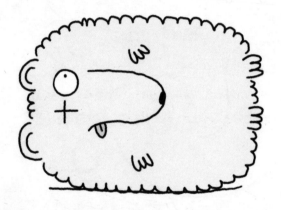

Miss Spivak looked at me. 'Is this true, Barry?' she asked, and I nodded, thinking back to all the times it had been, which was nine in case you'd forgotten.

'Waaah,' I cried, squeezing a fake tear out of my eyehole, trying to think of what to say next.

'This hamster,' said Miss Spivak, her eyes going all slitty. 'What was its name?'

Sharonella glared at me. 'Quick Bazzy, come up with one of your amazekeel names!' her eyes said.

Or maybe she just whispered it out of her mouth.

I crumpled my face up and flicked through my brain like it was a brochure for people looking for hamster names.

'Erm, Plurgle Flurgle?' I said. And even though I'd said 'erm' before it and put a question mark on the end, Miss Spivak nodded.

The bell for break started clanging and we headed out the door towards the playground.

'I'm sorry about Plurgle Flurgle, Barry,' called Miss Spivak.

'Thanks, Miss,' I said, feeling all sad. Even though the whole thing was comperleeterly made up.

Mogden School Tuck Shop

I spent the whole of Wednesday and Thursday screaming my head off at the Mogden Maniacs, trying to get them ready for the big match. Then all of a non-sudden it was Friday afternoon.

'So how we feeling about tomozzoid, Maniacs?' I said, bouncing the official Mogden Maniacs football up and down in the playground.

'Just chuck me the ball, Bus!' shouted Bunky, who was standing right in front of me. 'I've had enough of your bossing us around.'

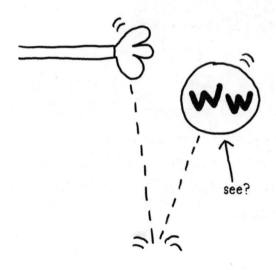

see?

I shook my head, wishing I'd never started calling Bunky 'Captain' in the first place.

'You really are getting too big for those boots of yours, aren't you?' I said, as Darren trudged towards Mogden School Tuck Shop.

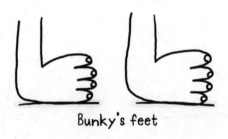

Bunky's feet

Bunky's boots

Mogden School Tuck Shop is the keel little tuck shop on the side of the playground that everyone's mums and dads are always trying to get shut down because all it sells is crisps and biscuits and fizzy drinks.

It's actukeely an old toilet block with a hole cut in the front of it that acts like a hatch.

Dolly the dinner dame was standing behind the counter, smiling like a really friendly, fat bollard.

'Gimme a Cherry Fronkle,' yawned Darren, handing her a golden coin.

'You look like you could do with a pick-me-up, love,' cooed Dolly, cracking open a can and plopping a straw into the little hole.

paper, of keelse →

'I'm pooped, Dolls,' drawled Darren, leaning against the counter, and he pulled Dazzy Rascal out of his pocket. 'This little fella's running me ragged.'

Dolly wiped the counter with a smelly old rag. 'I'll pretend I didn't see that,' she chuckled, and I stomped over to Darren, grabbing him by the collar.

119

'What d'you think you're doing, Darrenofski?' I whispered. 'You know these things are banned!'

I grabbed his Freakoid and chucked it back into my rucksack. 'That's the last time you'll see him before the game,' I said.

'Curse you, Loser!' cried Darren, sucking on his straw.

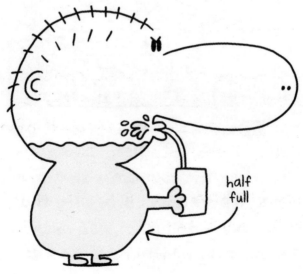

half full

Sharonella dug a hexagon-shaped coin out of her pocket. 'Packet of Thumb Sweets, Doll,' she said. 'Gotta keep me strength up for this stupid match.'

Dolly swooshed the crumply packet across the counter and Sharonella ripped it open, stuffing a couple of sugary thumbs into her cake hole.

'Ooh let's have one, Shaz,' smiled Bunky, jogging over.

'Uh, uh, uh,' I said, pushing his arm down. 'No more of that rubbish for my team. If the Mogden Maniacs are gonna win tomorrow you'll need to start watching what you eat.'

'Boo!' said Bunky as I snatched the packet of Thumb Sweets out of Sharonella's hand and pincered a couple, slotting them into my mouth.

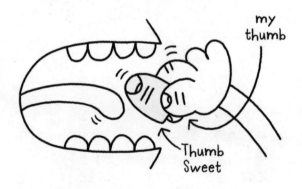

my thumb

Thumb Sweet

'Oi, I paid hard-earned cash for them things!' squawked Shazza.

'Yeah give it a rest, Barold,' sighed
Gordon. 'If Bunk fancies one of
Sharon's Thumb Sweets, let him
have it.'

I shook my head at Gordon. 'Firstly,
it's "Bunk-Y" to you,' I garbled, bits
of chewed-up Thumb Sweet
splattering out of my face hole.

'And secondly . . .' But I didn't have
a second point to make, so I couldn't
finish my sentence.

Bunky smiled at Smugly. 'Thank you, Gordon,' he said, trying to grab the packet out of my hand.

The crying sound from inside my rucksack was getting louder, but I was too annoyed to notice.

'Gimme that blooming can!' I boomed, snatching Darren's Fronkle out of his trotter. 'Chip Snyder's Top Tip number eighty-eight: No carbonated beverages for people with crocodile-shaped faces.'

in his Fronkle swamp

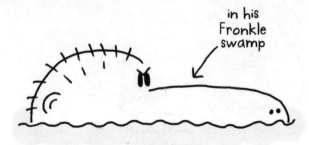

'Well now you're just making them up,' said Stuart, and Darren nodded.

'He's losing it, Shmendrix,' he said. 'The kid's not fit to be Coach!'

I Pain-au-Choc'ed on the spot until I was facing Darren. 'Oh yeah?' I growled. 'Well YOU'RE not fit to be a Mogden Maniac!'

'Yes he is,' said Bunky. 'And by the way, Barry, I was the one who came up with that name.'

I twizzled round on the spot again. Something about Bunky calling me by my real-life name was making me feel dizzy.

Or maybe it was all that twizzling.

'Right, that's it!' I cried, whipping my rucksack off my back and slinging it to the ground.

'Careful, Loser!' shrieked Bunky. 'The you-know-whats are in there!'

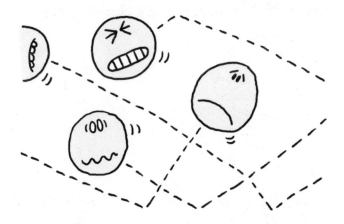

But I didn't even care. 'I've had enough of your cheek, "Captain"!' I shouted. 'Just because you can kick a ball in a straight line doesn't mean you can talk to me like I'm a comperleet idiot.'

'YOU can talk!' cried Bunky. 'You're the one who's been bossing us about all week!'

Darren nodded. 'It's true, Loser,' he burped. "Snot exactly like we asked you to be our coach in the first place, was it?'

'You wouldn't even be a proper team if it wasn't for me!' I cried.

'But we didn't WANT to be a proper team, Bazzy,' said Sharonella. 'We were happy just knocking the ball around.'

better times

'Shazza's right,' said Stuart, doing a blow off. 'The last thing I want to do this Saturday is play the Green Giants. Saturdays are my relaxing day. How can I relax when I'm running around on a football pitch? It's just not relaxing!'

Nancy was standing nearby, measuring the height of Dolly's tuck shop. 'Nancy, you're a sensible young lady,' I said. 'Tell this lot they're being stupid.'

Nancy jotted down a number in her notebook and looked up. 'Sorry Baz,' she said. 'But you can't force people to do something they don't wanna do . . .'

My nose drooped, like there was
a Crying-Freakoid-sized bogie
stuck inside it somewhere near the
nostril end.

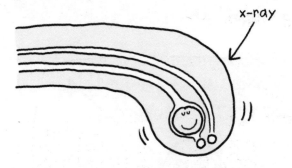

x-ray

'FINE,' I muttered, preparing to
activate Operation Pain au Chocolat.
Only this time, I wouldn't be twizzling
back round again.

I reached down to pick my rucksack
up, then remembered what was
inside. I unzipped it and pulled out the
wailing box.

'Barry,' whispered Dolly. 'Be careful!'
But it was already too late.

'I suppose you'll be wanting your
Crying Freakoids back,' I said, holding
the box up in the air.

The sound of an evil bollard click-
clacking up behind me got louder
and louder, then stopped.

CLICK!
CLACK!

'I've got you this time!' screeched
a familikeels old voice as a walking
stick tapped me on the shoulder.

Saying goodbye

'I can't believe Queenie confiscated our Crying Freakoids,' said Stuart as the Mogden Maniacs headed out through the gates after school.

'Thanks for reminding us, Shmendrix,' said Gordon.

I was walking behind them with
Nancy, who was the only one I could
be sure didn't toterally hate me.

'What're we gonna DO?' blubbered
Sharonella. She'd been blubbering like
that ever since Queenie had click-
clacked off with my shoe box.

'Ooh, I can just picture them now –
stuffed in some stinky old drawer,
crying themselves to death,' cooed
Darren, sounding like an old granny.

Nancy, who was jotting down the height of Mrs Cornichon the lollipop lady's lollipop stick, pushed her glasses up her nose. 'How long DO they live for without patting?' she asked.

Nancy's notebook

'Nobody's comperleeterly sure,' I said, not looking up. I itched my bum and blinked, trying not to imagine what poor little Barry Junior and his pals were going through somewhere deep inside the depths of Mogden School's staff room.

'Surely there's something we can
do to get them back, Bunk?' said
Gordon.

Bunky shook his head. He was walking
next to Gordon, and I wondered if
maybe they were actual real-life best
friends now. 'It's no good, Gord,' he
said. 'Once that old dinner dame's got
her mitts on something, it's toast.'

Barry
Junior
now

I flicked through my brain, looking for a way to say sorry. 'Don't worry team,' I mumbled. 'Coach Barry'll think of something.'

'You're not our coach anymore, Barry,' said Stuart, but not in a mean way, just as if it was a fact.

Sharonella rotated ninety degrees to the left then headed down her road, like a stray tray of pain au chocs. 'No hard feelings, Bazzy,' she said, not looking me in the eye.

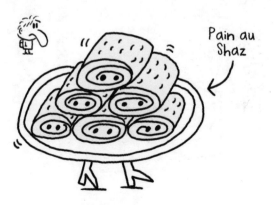

Pain au Shaz

137

'Thanks a lot, Loser,' said Darren, waddling up to his front door.

'See you later Bunky and Nancy,' said Gordon, as him and Stuart walked off towards their houses.

Then it was just me, Bunky and Nancy.

We got to the end of my road and I looked up at my best friends through the tears in my eyes.

windscreen wipers

'Seriously, don't worry about it, Barry' said Nancy. Probably because she didn't have a Crying Freakoid in the first place.

But Bunky didn't look so relaxed.

He started to walk off, then stopped, and for a millisecond I thought he might turn around.

But he just kept on going.

Oo-ooh

'Oo-ooh love!' cooed my mum as I walked through the front door and traipsed into the living room, feeling like I was dying.

'Oo-ooh,' I sighed, slumping onto the sofa and opening the laptop, immedi-Smoogling Crying Freakoids, wondering if I should buy a brand new one and start all over again, the way you do with hamsters.

HALF PRICE!

Just then the front door opened.
'Oo-ooh!' called my dad.

'Oo-ooh, Kenneth!' cried my mum.
'How was the course today - any
better?'

I rewound my brain to Monday,
replaying their boring chat about him
doing team-building exercises with the
other losers from his work.

learning to
trust

'You know what?' said my dad, collapsing onto the sofa. 'It was actually pretty fun!'

'Fun,' I muttered to myself, trying to remember what the word even meant. 'Ha, that's all over for me now.'

Only a couple of days before I'd had my whole life ahead of me - Barry Junior in my pocket and my best friend by my side . . .

Now what did I have? I was a washed-up football coach with the blood of six Crying Freakoids on his hands.

'Go on then Ken, tell us what you got up to!' warbled my mum, coming into the front room carrying a tray of Feeko's chocolate digestives, just like the other day.

My dad stroked the bit of his chin
where his beard'd be if he didn't
shave the next morning. 'Well,' he
said. 'Everyone wrote down what
they were good at on a giant pad.'

pad probably
wasn't this
big

My mum crunched on a biccy and
I wondered if this was what being
a grown-up was like – getting all
excited listening to a boring old story
about people scribbling on a piece
of paper.

'Then we took all the things we were good at and added them together,' he carried on. 'And we sort of created this super-human person who had all our skills in one body!'

probably didn't look like this

I pressed the mute button on the remote control, hoping maybe it'd shut my dad up. But it didn't, so I un-muted the telly and turned the volume up to fifty.

'It really taught me a lesson,' shouted my dad over the TV.

'What was that, love?' asked my mum, reaching for another biscuit.

My dad smiled like he was a presenter on a TV programme who was about to say the most important bit in the whole show.

MOGDEN TV

'The lesson it taught me,' he said,
'was that a group of people will
always be stronger if they work
together as a team!'

'Fascinating stuff,' said my mum,
biscuit crumbs spraying out of her
cake hole.

all over
me

'Oh yeah, REALLY interestikeels,'
I muttered. 'NOT!'

My dad leaned over and started to tickle me, but I didn't laugh.

'What's wrong with my grumpy little Loser?' he asked.

'You don't even wanna know,' I said. Then I told them anyway.

'Hmm,' said my mum once I'd finished explaining, which was about half an hour later. 'I think I might've had one of my brilliant and amazing ideas.'

'You have those too?' I asked,
reaching for a Feeko's chocolate
digestive, but the plate was empty.

Desmond crawled into my mum's lap
and scrunched his face up like a
Crying Freakoid doing a poo.

NNNG!

'Oui, oui, Barry!' smiled my mum, and
she handed Des to my dad. 'Change
this one's nappy while I talk to my big
boy, would you Ken?'

Saturday school

'This'd better be good, Barold,' said Gordon Smugly the next day. 'The World Cup final's on in an hour, you know.'

It was Saturday morning and we were all standing outside the school gates.

I'd been lying awake thinking about my mum's idea all night and had only just phoned the Mogden Maniacs ten minutes earlier.

'Thanks for coming at such short notice,' I said. 'I know I'm the last person you want to see, but we don't have a lot of time.'

Nancy whipped her measuring tape out and jotted down the length of a passing cat.

'As you know, our dearly beloved Crying Freakoids were cruelly snatched from our bosoms yesterday break-time,' I started.

'Bosoms!' sniggled Stuart.

'Without us there to pat their little heads every time they start to blubber, our sweet babies won't have long on this earth,' I carried on.

'Get to the point, Barry,' said Nancy.

'Now as I see it, we have two options - either we let Barry Junior and the rest of them die somewhere inside a smelly old drawer . . .' I paused, letting them imagine what I'd just said.

'Or we go get them.'

Darren stretched his arms out and yawned. 'Laying it on a bit thick ain'tcha, Loser?' he said, and Shaz, who was still wearing her dressing gown and slippers, gave him a nudge.

DONK!

'Let's give him a chance shall we, Daz?' she said, and she turned to me, her eyes red from crying all night. 'Bazzy baby, tell me you've got a plan.'

Number one skills

I whipped a piece of paper out of my pocket and unfolded it.

'What in the name of unkeelness is that?' burped Darren.

'It's a piece of paper, Darren,' I said, pulling a pen out from behind my ear.

'Okay, but how's that going to get me my Lil Gordy back?' sneered Gordon.

I dropped to my knees and flattened the paper out on the pavement. 'Nancy, what do you reckon you're best at out of everything in the whole wide world?' I asked.

594mm

'Huh?' said Nancy, who'd kneeled down next to me and was measuring the piece of paper.

'That's it!' I said, writing down her name and the words 'Measuring stuff' after it. 'Okay, Darren next - what's your number one skill?'

Stuart itched his nose. 'No offence Barry, but what's this all about?'

doing their skills

'Just trust me for a minute, would you?' I said, peering up at Dazza, who was cracking open a can of Fronkle.

'Got it!' I said, writing 'Slurping Fronkle' next to his name on the piece of paper.

Next I turned to Sharonella. 'You're easy too,' I said, writing her name then the word 'Nattering' next to it.

'Bunky, your turn,' I said, peeking up at him. It was the first time I'd looked at him properly since we'd arrived, and I felt my cheeks go red like Desmond's when he does his poos.

'Keepy uppies, of keelse,' said Bunky.
'I'm the keelest at keepy uppies.'

'Glad to see those boots of yours
haven't got any bigger,' I said, and he
sniggled, but only for a snigglisecond.

'What about you, Smugly?' I asked.

'Most things,' said Gordon. 'But if I
had to choose a number one thing
it'd probably be . . .' he scratched a
spot on the end of his nose. 'Looking
after number one!'

I wrote that down next to his name. 'Yeah that makes sense,' I said. 'But it isn't much use when you're trying to build a team.'

Stuart did a blow off. 'When are you gonna learn, Barry?' he sighed. 'We don't want to be in your team!'

Stuart's fart

'Don't worry, Stuey,' I said. 'This is something different. Now, what shall I write next to you?'

Gordon put his hand on Stuart's shoulder. 'I can take care of this, Shmendrix,' he said. 'Stuart is good at whatever I tell him to be good at.'

I looked at Stuart and he shrugged. 'Come on Stuey,' said Darren. 'Don't let Smugly boss you around like that!'

'Dazzy's right, Stu,' cooed Sharonella. 'Stand up for yourself, man!'

feeling the pressure

Stuart peered up at Gordon, then round at the team. 'Erm . . .' he said, trying to think of his skill.

'Have a think about it,' I said, standing up and slotting the pen back behind my ear.

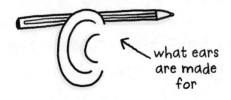

what ears are made for

'Wait a minute Bazzy,' said Shaz. 'You haven't written down **YOUR** number one skill yet!'

'I'm the one whose mum came up with the brilliant and amazekeel idea!' I smiled, getting ready to tell them what it was.

Team building

'So let me get this straight,' said Bunky. 'You want us to sneak into Mogden School's staff room and rescue the Crying Freakoids?'

'Yep,' I said.

Stuart blew off. 'B-but how?' he stuttered.

'By adding all our number one skills together into one great big super-human person!' I smiled.

Darren
Bunky
Shaz
Gordon
me
Nancy
Stuart

'O-kaaay,' said Nancy, pushing her glasses up her nose. 'And you say your mum came up with this idea?'

'She thought up the team-building bit,' I said. 'Everything else was mine!'

'But what about Queenie?' said Sharonella, pointing at the gates of Mogden School. 'That miserable old dinner dame lives through there, remember?'

'And Mr Walbyoff too,' said Bunky.

Stuart glanced up at the gates. 'How are we gonna get through them?' he said. 'They're chained shut!'

'Nancy, how high do you reckon those things are?' I said as we all stood there staring at the gates.

Mogden Zoo

Nancy whipped out her tape measure and held it up against the gates. 'Too high for us to get over,' she said.

'Oh well this is just brillikeels,' said Bunky. 'Come on Barry, you're the one who dragged us out here first thing on a Saturday morning - what are we gonna do now?'

'Yeah Loser,' said Darren. 'I could be lying naked in bed drinking Fronkle.'

'What?' said Dazza. 'You don't drink Fronkle in bed?'

Just then a horrible little bollard waddled into the corner of my eye.

'Duck!' I cried.

'Where?' said Stuart.

'Get down!' I whisper-shouted, and we all ducked. 'It's Queenie – I just spotted her patrolling the playground.'

Sharonella shook her head. 'Doesn't that dame ever give up?'

'Hey, that gives me an idea,' said Nancy, and I Pain-au-Choc'ed my head round to face her. 'Queenie **MUST** have to leave the school sometimes - to get down the shops and stuff.'

'So?' said Gordon, his lanky legs bent in two.

'So there must be another way in,' said Nancy. 'A separate gate just for Queenie and Mr Walbyoff to use.'

I clicked my fingers and pointed at Nancy. 'Verkenwerken, I think you might've cracked it!'

Revenge of the squirrel

We waddle-ducked out of view of the front gates then straightened up. 'Follow me,' I cried over my shoulder, starting to circle the school, looking for a different way in.

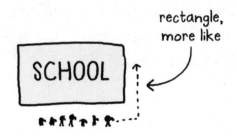

rectangle, more like

SCHOOL

'It's no use, we'll never find it,'
panted Stuart ten billiseconds later.
We'd only run about a metre, but
he was already comperleeterly out
of breath.

He leaned against a wooden fence
to catch his breath. 'Hey, maybe my
number one skill is finding fences to
lean against?' he grinned.

'Do be quiet, Shmendrix,' snapped
Gordon, shoving Stuart out of the
way and leaning against the fence
instead. 'Waaahhh!' he cried, as it
creaked open behind him to reveal a
hidden alleyway.

'That wasn't a fence,' gasped Bunky, darting down it. 'It was a secret gate!'

The alleyway opened out onto the back playing field of Mogden School. Just across it you could see Queenie and Mr Walbyoff's bungalow, which was the shape of a shoebox only a hundred times bigger.

'Keep low,' I said, starting to duck-run across the field like I'd just got out of a helicopter and didn't want my head getting chopped off by the blades.

We came to a stop behind a wall
next to the main foyer of the school.
A tall pine tree towered above us,
and a cone dropped out of it,
doinking Darren on the head.

BONK!

'Ouch!' he whisper-screamed, as a
familikeels-looking squirrel leapt
from a branch onto the ground.

'Hey little squizzle,' nattered
Sharonella. 'Come over here and
give your Auntie Shaz a cuddle!'

The squirrel's nose twitched. 'Here,
squizzie-squizzle,' said Shazza,
carrying on nattering, and the furry
little rodent inched away until it was
in front of the automatic doors of
the foyer.

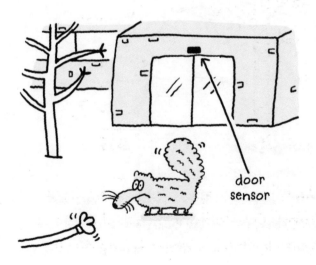

door
sensor

Swoosh!

'They're turned on!' I gasped, as the glass doors slid open. 'Quick, let's get inside before anyone spots us.'

I dived towards the foyer, forward-rolling like Future Ratboy, and immedi-hid behind a big stand-up cork board with paintings of trees stapled all over the front of it.

Everything went quiet. 'Bit weird being here at the weekend innit,' nattered Sharonella, and I shushed her.

'What's that noise?' I whispered, hearing a tiny little banging sound. I popped my head round the cork board and spotted Mr Walbyoff's doll's-house-sized model of Mogden Town.

There, huddled behind it, was the top of Mr Walbyoff's head.

Mr Walbyoff was sitting on a fold-up stool, holding the tiniest hammer I'd ever seen, which he was banging against a miniature house's roof.

'Aw, isn't he sweet,' whispered Shaz. 'Working on his little model - makes you wanna cry, dunnit.'

I thought of Barry Junior and the other Crying Freakoids weeping in their drawer and I took a deep breath so I wouldn't start sobbing too.

'This is no time for tears, Shaz,' I said.
'We need to get past Walbyoff and
up the stairs to the staff room.'

The automatic doors swooshed open
and an evil bollard stepped through.

Queenie   bollard

'There you are Dennis,' growled
Queenie, and Mr Walbyoff looked up.
'Shoulda guessed you'd be tinkering
with your stupid little doll's house.'

'It's not a doll's house,' said the caretaker. 'It's a scale model of Mogden Town.'

'It's a waste of blooming time, that's what it is,' snapped Queenie. 'Anyway, you want a cuppa?'

dinner dame style →

Mr Walbyoff nodded. 'Yes please love,' he said, standing up all stiffly. 'Think I'll pop to the toilet for a wizzle first though.'

'It's your life,' said Queenie, waddling off towards the canteen like she owned the place.

'Quick, this is our chance!' I whisper-shouted, and we all darted towards the stairs.

Staff room

The door to the staff room creaked open.

'So this is where Miss Spivak disappears off to at break times,' said Bunky, as we wandered in.

Squishy square seats were lined up all round the edge, apart from one whole wall which'd been turned into a sort of mini kitchen with a fridge, sink and microwave oven.

'Ooh, this is so naughty,' said
Sharonella, retying her dressing
gown and glancing around. 'I love it!'

A thirsty-looking spider plant sat
on top of a beige filing cabinet in
the corner of the room. I headed
towards it. 'Drawers,' I said, starting
to pull the top one open. 'Look in
all the drawers.'

'Nothing in this one,' called Gordon, rifling through a little wooden cabinet filled to the brim with mini staplers.

'Zilchoid,' said Darren, poking his nose into a metal tray overflowing with rubber bands and paperclips and chewed-up biro lids.

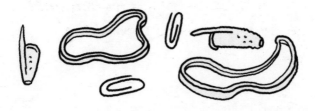

'Barry Junior?' I called, listening out for his cry. I pulled the bottom drawer of the filing cabinet open but all it had inside were a couple of boring old scratched-up sellotape dispensers without any sellotape in them. 'Where ARE you?'

182

'They've GOT to be in here somewhere,' said Bunky. 'Maybe there's a secret compartment?'

I clicked my fingers and pointed at him. 'Good thinking, Bunky,' I said. 'Nancy, you keep guard. Shazza, Dazza, start looking behind all the chairs - maybe there's a hidden door in one of the walls or something.'

hidden
door

Stuart and Gordon walked up to me. 'What shall we do?' they asked.

'Check the cupboards,' I said. 'Leave no stone unturned.'

'I don't think there'll be any stones Barry,' said Stuart.

'Shut up Shmendrix,' said Gordon, heading towards the kitchen.

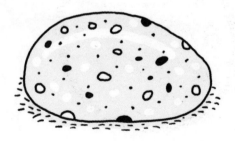

Group hug

The second hand of the clock on the staff room wall tick-tocked round in a circle ten times.

'Argh, this is useless!' I cried. 'We've been looking for AGES.'

'Still nothing,' said Stuart, who'd found half a packet of Thumb Sweets under the sink and was chewing on one now, the nail bit sticking out of his mouth like he was finishing eating a whole person.

inside

Thumb Sweet

'Maybe it's time we face the facts,' said Nancy from the doorway. 'Those Crying Freakoids have probably been dead for hours anyway.'

I dropped to my knees and stretched my hands out towards the strip-lights screwed into the ceiling tiles above. **'NOOO!!!'** I cried.

this looks familikeels

Shaz put her hand on my shoulder. 'I know, Bazzy,' she whimpered. 'It breaks my heart to think of poor old Mini Shaz crying for her Mumma.'

'We'll never forget those little fellas,' said Bunky, and Darren nodded, a Fronkle tear dribbling out of his eye and down his cheek, into his mouth.

Dazzy
Rascal

Gordon's bottom lip started to quiver and Stuart peered up at his boss, his eyeballs glistening.

'Come over here you big softies,'
called Sharonella, and Smugly and
Shmendrix ran over, and we all had a
mahoosive granny hug.

'At least we have each other, eh?'
warbled Gordon. Nancy coughed
and we all looked up.

'Erm, I hate to break up the group
hug,' she said, 'but shouldn't we be
thinking about getting the keelness
out of here before Queenie finds us?'

The tiny little tuck shop

We tiptoed down the stairs, peering through the bannister.

'Where's Mr Walbyoff?' whispered Stuart.

I zoomed in on the old caretaker's fold-up stool and spotted a full cup of tea steaming on the table in front of it.

'Maybe he's still in the toilet,' said Shazza.

'Let's just get the keelness out of here while we still can,' I said.

'Good idea, Coach,' said Bunky, giving me an upside-down-reverse salute, and we carried on to the bottom of the stairs and millimetred past Mr Walbyoff's model of Mogden Town.

Nancy stopped and pointed to a tiny little bin. 'Hey, I measured that!' she smiled.

tiny rubbish inside

'Congrats,' said Gordon. 'You must be very proud.'

I looked at the bin, which was sitting just outside a miniature version of the school tuck shop.

I bent over and peered into the tiny old toilet block, recognising the serving hatch on the front.

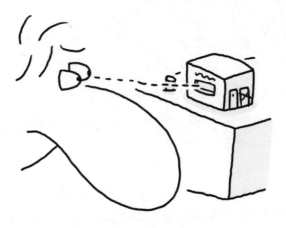

And that's when I spotted it.

Dinner dames only

'What is it, Bazzy?' gasped Shazza, catching me as I stumbled backwards, falling into her arms.

I pointed at the little model of the tuck shop. 'H-how did I never spot it before?'

I scrabbled to my feet and we all peered through the little hatch in the front of the miniature sweetie store.

'What's he talking about now?' said Darren.

I pointed at a tiny door on the back wall of the doll's-house-sized tuck shop with a minuscule sign above it. The sign read: 'Dinner Ladies Only'.

'A secret staff room just for dinner dames?' said Sharonella, as a silhouette of an old caretaker appeared in the window of the door leading off towards the gents toilets.

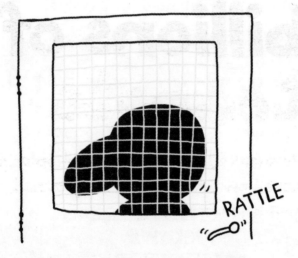

'It's Mr Walbyoff - he's back!' whispered Bunky.

'Quick, to the tuck shop!' I said, as we zoomed through the automatic doors.

Millions & billions of teapots

We sneaked up to the tuck shop and pushed on the side door. It groaned open and we stepped inside.

'Look at all those Thumb Sweets!' drooled Shazza, and I bonked her on the head.

'Concentrate, Shaz,' I said, pointing at the secret door on the back wall.

'It's boiling in here!' whispered Stuart as we crept through it, peering around.

The dinner dame room was half the size of the staff room but the chairs were twice as big. They all had high backs with doilies draped over the tops of them and the carpet was as thick as the grass in Mogden Park.

'Teapots . . .' gasped Shazza, pointing at a row of them, all wrapped up warm in woollen cosies. 'Millions and billions of teapots.'

In the corner of the room a wooden-sided TV was playing an old black and white movie. On top of it, three brightly coloured toys were lined up like tiny prisoners.

all from Future Ratboy

199

'Hey, that's Jocelyn Twiggs's Not Bird!' whisper-cried Darren, pointing at a cuddly little brown bird, and I rewound my brain to the time Queenie snatched it off him for carving 'Twiggs' into the big tree in the corner of the playground.

'And there's Tracy Pilchard's Jamjar figure,' said Sharonella, pointing at a plastic figure of a girl with five arms.

Not Bird

Jamjar

A strange noise, sort of like a bollard snoring, floated through the hot, thick air over from the other side of the room, and we all jumped.

look like
action figures

'W-what in the name of . . .' whispered Bunky, not finishing his sentence, and I peered into the darkest corner of the room.

Sleeping bollard

'Qu-Qu-Qu-Qu-Queenie!' I whisper-stutter-screamed.

There, squidged into a granny seat, sat the evilest dinner dame in Mogden Town, her feet up on a poufe and a familikeels-looking shoebox in her lap.

'Shhh,' shushed Stuart. 'She's asleep. Hey, maybe that's my number one skill - noticing that dinner dames are asleep!'

'Oh yeah, very useful,' whisper-
snapped Gordon, and he bonked
Stuart on the head.

'Barry Junior?' I called in my quietest
voice, and I heard a tiny cry.

'His batteries are low,' said Bunky.
'We don't have long.'

'Mini Shaz?' whispered Sharonella.
'Can you hear me, baby? It's Mumma
- I'm here to rescue you!'

Mini   Mumma

Mini Shaz whined quietly in Queenie's
lap, and the dinner dame shifted in
her seat.

I looked round at my friends and got
ready to do my best Coach Barry
voice. 'Prepare yourselves, team,'
I said. 'We're going in.'

Nose brushing

Have you ever reached your arms out to grab a shoebox-full of Crying Freakoids from the lap of a sleeping bollard?

It's not as easy as it sounds - especially when your nose is as long as mine.

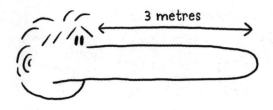

3 metres

'Watch out Barry, you're brushing her hooter with your shnozzle,' whispered Shazza.

'Don't breathe out,' said Nancy. 'The air from your nostrils'll wake her up.'

SNORE!

'Try not to wobble the shoebox too much,' said Darren. 'You don't wanna make all the Crying Freakoids cry at once.'

'Can you all stop telling me what to do,' I hissed through my teeth. 'This is hard enough as it is!'

I peered down into the shoebox, which was rising up and down with Queenie's breath. 'You okay, little fellas?' I whispered.

It was hard to tell – for all I knew, half of them were goners already.

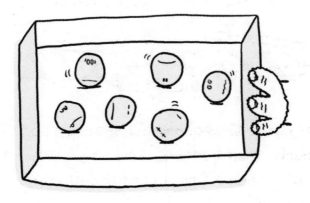

Queenie's wrinkly old paw looked like it had a pret-ty tight grip on the box. 'My hands are shaking,' I whispered over my shoulder. 'I dunno if I can do it.'

Darren clicked his fingers. 'I've got it!' he said, whipping a straw out of his pocket.

'Got what - a straw?' said Stuart.

'Well yeah,' said Darren, and I zoomed in on it – it was the one Dolly had plonked into his Fronkle yesterday. 'But I've also got an idea!' He stuck the straw into his mouth. 'Remember what my number one skill was?' he asked.

'Slurping Fronkle?' I whispered.

'Not just Fronkle,' said Darren,
shoving me out of the way and
dangling his straw over the shoe box.
'Watch this!'

He sucked through the straw and the
Crying Freakoids started to wobble.

Plunk!

Barry Junior floated a millimetre off the bottom of the box, then shot up and suckered himself to the end of Darren's straw.

'He's got one!' cried Bunky.

'Hey, how come Barry's goes first?' whispered Gordon, as Darren twizzled slowly round and stopped sucking, my Crying Freakoid plunking into my held-out hand.

'You wanna come up here and do this, Smugly?' snapped Darrenofski, and Queenie breathed out, her lips fluttering like curtains in the smelly breeze.

stinks of tea

Next Darren suckered Bunky Two, passing him to Bunky One.

'You alright, boy?' said Bunky, cupping him in his hands, and I heard a tiny little electronic squeak, then the sound of my best friend holding in a sob. 'He's still alive!'

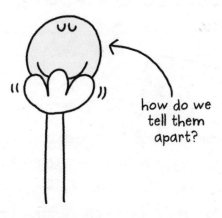

how do we tell them apart?

'Shazza,' garbled Darren through his straw, and he dropped Mini Shaz into her palm.

Queenie's belly rumbled and the shoebox tipped to one side, the rest of the Crying Freakoids rolling to that end.

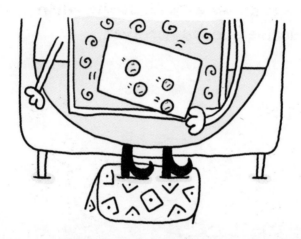

Darren sucked his Freakoid out of the box, slipping it into his pocket. 'Hurry up Darrenofski,' said Gordon, and Darrenofski suckered Stuey No Legs out, just to teach the Smugmeister a lesson.

'Okay, I deserved that,' said Gordon, and Darren was just about to suck Lil Gordy up with his straw when Queenie opened her eyes.

PLINK   PLINK

Bouncy castle bum

'Dennis, is that you?' warbled Queenie, scrabbling around for her glasses. She knocked them off the little round table next to her chair and they landed in the long grass of the carpet.

'Let's get out of here!' whispered Shazza.

Gordon yelped. 'B-but Lil Gordy – Queenie's still got him!'

Queenie started to heave herself out of her chair, the shoebox tilting on her lap.

Darren's mouth gaped open and his straw fell out, disappearing into the grass. 'I-I can't see it,' he cried.

Stuart stepped forward. 'I've got it!' he whisper-cried.

'The straw?' whispered Gordon.

'No, my number one skill,' said Stuart. 'Invisibility!'

not invisible at all

He strode up to Queenie, his nostrils a millimetre away from her crusted-up old shnoz-holes, and reached his hand out to grab Lil Gordy from the box.

Queenie's eyeballs creaked in their sockets as they zoomed in on Stuart's face. **'Waaahhh!!!'** she screamed, leaping out of her seat. 'It's a blooming kiddywinkle!'

'Lil Gordy!' cried Shazza, as the Crying Freakoid shot into the sky. She ran towards it, headering it by accident.

FWOOSH!

'Look at him go!' gasped Nancy, as the little ball rainbowed across the room, rebounded off a teapot and headed straight towards my hooter.

'Not my prize-winning shnozzle!' I screamed, Pain-au-Choc-ing round on the spot, and Lil Gordy boinged off my bum like it was a bouncy castle blown up by blow offs.

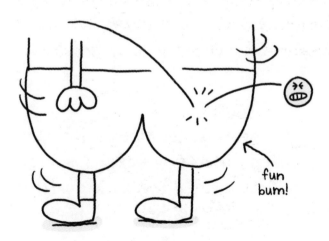

fun bum!

Bunky dived forward, stuck his foot out and caught the naughty little Freakoid before it fell into the long grass. 'Check this out!' he whisper-sniggled, keepy-uppy-ing Lil Gordy while twizzling round.

DONK DONK

'You lot are in serious trouble!' screeched Queenie, swivelling her head like a dinosaur and knocking a packet of biscuits off the shelf with her enormous wrinkly hooter.

'Heads up, Smugly!' shouted Bunky, kicking Lil Gordy into the air, and Gordon forward-rolled across the floor, sprung to his feet, did a triple-reverse-upside-down salute to himself and caught the Crying Freakoid in his mouth.

What now?

'I think we lost her!' sniggled Shaz as we zoomed out of Mogden School and ran up the road, skidding to a stop round a corner.

Nancy patted Stuart on the back. 'Looks like your skill is waking up dinner dames,' she chuckled.

Gordon laughed. 'Thanks for sucking all our Freakoids out of that shoe box, Darren,' he said, wiping the spit off his one.

SQUEAK

SQUEAK

'Don't thank me,' said Darren. 'It was Bunky who saved Lil Gordy.'

Bunky pointed at me. 'Bazza came up with the amazekeel plan,' he smiled.

I patted the piece of paper in my pocket. 'We all played our part,' I said in my Chip Snyder voice.

223

'Ooh, Mumma's SO happy to see her little baby!' squealed Sharonella, rocking Mini Shaz in her arms.

'Sooo . . .' said Nancy, trying to change the subject. 'What are you lot up to for the rest of the day?'

A blow-off squeaked out of my bum and I gasped, which is never a good idea if you've just done a fart.

comes out here

goes back in here

'Oh my unkeelness, I comperleeterly forgot to cancel our game against the Green Giants!' I cried.

Gordon looked at his watch. 'What time did you say it was again?' he asked, even though I hadn't said it in the first place.

'Half past eleven,' I said, and every one of the Mogden Maniacs, Nancy Verkenwerken included, smiled at me.

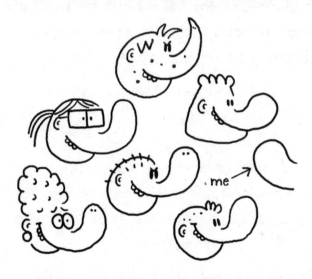

.me →

'Looks like we can still make it if we hurry,' grinned Captain Bunky.

Avocado Hill Stadium

'Maybe we'll let Nancy look after the Freakoids this time,' chuckled Bunky as we walked through the gates into Avocado Hill Stadium.

The crowd cheered and I spotted Jocelyn Twiggs sitting next to the rest of our class, along with Miss Spivak and Dolly the dinner dame too.

'Did you hear?' called Jocelyn. 'Smeldovia won the World Cup!'

'Oh my unkeelness!' I smiled. We'd been so busy with our team building exercise, I'd comperleeterly forgotten about the World Cup final.

couldn't fit on page

GO MOGDEN MANIACS!

The Green Giants were warming up on the side of the pitch. 'Ready for a whipping, Mogden Midgets?' smiled Tarquin, stretching his leg against a dinner dame, I mean a bollard.

'I wouldn't be so cocky if I were you,'
said Nancy, giving Mini Shaz and Lil
Gordy a cuddle. 'Anything Chip
Snyder can do, Coach Loser can
do better!'

'Listen team,' I said, getting the
Maniacs into a huddle and staring
them in the eyes, Chip Snyder-style.
'I know we've been through a lot
these past few days . . .'

Sharonella's eyeballs welled up. 'Don't go all mushy on us now, Baz,' she warbled, whipping a football card out of her hand and passing it to me. 'Here, you look after Ronaldio for me while I'm out there.'

I took the card and slotted it into my pocket. 'Fair enough, Shaz,' I said. 'Just enjoy yourselves, okay?'

Bunky nodded. 'Sure thing, Coach,' he smiled, as the whistle blew.

The big game

'Come on you Maniacs!' screamed Nancy nineteen minutes later. There was a minute left in the game and the score was five all.

'Blimey Nance, you've changed your tune!' I chuckled, looking across at her.

She was standing on the sidelines cuddling all six of the Crying Freakoids, jumping up and down like Chip Snyder except without the moustache.

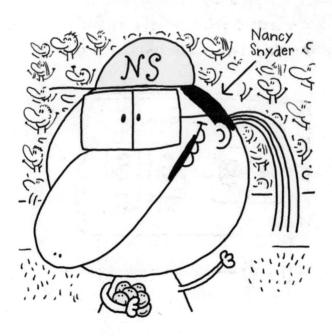

Nancy Snyder

'Ooh, foul!' she shouted, and I Pain-au-Choc'ed my head back round to the pitch. Stuart Shmendrix was lying on the grass, his face scrunched up like Barry Junior when he needs his bum wiped.

Bunky glanced up at me and frowned. 'Doesn't look good, Coach,' he mouthed.

'Darren, you stay centre!' I boomed. 'Shazza, keep your eye on Tarquin.'

Gordon, who was in goal, shook his head. 'We can't play with four,' he said.

I ran onto the pitch, straight up to Stuart. 'How you doing, little Stuey?' I asked.

'Don't . . . think . . . I'm . . . gonna . . . make . . . it . . .' croaked Stuart.

'Okay let's take you off,' I said, heaving him up with Bunky and carrying him to the edge of the pitch.

We lowered him down next to Nancy. 'Verkenwerken, you're up,' I said.

'Huh?' said Nancy. 'Oh-ho-no! I've got these little fellas to look after. Besides, I'm still not **THAT** into football.'

The Crying Freakoids wailed and Bunky ruffled my hair. 'Come on Baz,' he said, nodding at the pitch. 'There's only a minute left . . .'

'Hurry up, you midgets!' cried Tarquin, as I shook my head.

'You've got to be kidding, Bunk,'
I warbled. 'I can't even kick a ball
straight!'

Bunky shrugged. 'Who cares,' he said.
'It's only football. Besides, you might
surprise yourself!'

Barry the Maniac

'I can't believe I'm doing this,' I said, bending down to tie up my shoelaces. I patted my pockets and pulled out Sharonella's card.

Ronaldio Donaldio's face smiled out of it and I glanced down at his Top Tip for how to be a keel player:

'Don't overthink it!'

I looked up at Bunky, who was standing in the middle of the pitch waiting for his best friend to join him.

His eyes were focused on the bit of air in front of his nostrils and his tongue was half hanging out of his mouth, sort of like a dog's.

'Oh my unkeelness,' I gasped to myself, suddenkeely realising why he was so good at football. 'It's his tiny little brain - he isn't thinking about anything else at all!'

I passed the football card to Nancy and jogged onto the grass. 'One minute left, fellas,' called the referee, and he blew his whistle.

The end

Final score:
Mogden Maniacs 5
Green Giants   6

(Own goal off Loser's nose).

About the author and drawer

Jim Smith is the keelest kids' book author and drawer in the whole wide world amen.

He graduated from art school with first-class honours (the best you can get) and went on to create the branding for a keel little chain of coffee shops.

He's also designed cards and gifts under the name Waldo Pancake.

Nothing else has ever happened to him.

waiting for → something